This book belongs to

Violet Elizabeth
Jane Pavitt
2010

Age **2**

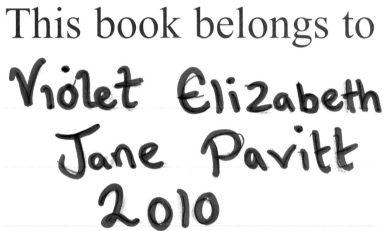

BEDTIME STORIES

©2006 Alligator Books Limited

Published by Alligator Books Limited
Gadd House, Arcadia Avenue
London N3 2JU

Printed in China

Daisy's First Adventure

On Sunday mornings when Sam and Sara went to the park, Sara always took her doll Daisy along with her.

Now, although Daisy didn't want to be left at home, she did find her trips to the park rather boring.

While Sam and Sara played ball Daisy was left lying in the grass looking up at the sky, and when they played hide-and-seek or climbed trees, Daisy was left alone propped up in the corner of a hard park bench.

"I wish I could go round the park instead of staying in one place all the time," the doll thought to herself… and on this Sunday morning Daisy was about to get her wish!

There were times when Sara's brother, Sam, could be quite a naughty boy, and as they ran across the park, he snatched Sara's doll and hurled her high into the air.

"Something exciting is happening to me at last!" gasped Daisy as she flew over the trees. Down below she could see children sailing toy boats on the lake, people were cycling and skating and jogging round the park, and everybody was having so much fun.

All of a sudden, Daisy was lifted up in the fluttering tails of a passing kite. A strong gust of wind took her all the way round the park, and as she looked down, she saw Sam and Sara searching for her in the long grass by the trees. The next moment the wind dropped, the kite fluttered and dived down towards the lake. But just before it hit the water, Daisy let go of the kite tails and jumped onto the deck of a toy sailing boat.

"That was lucky," Daisy giggled to herself as she sped across the water. It was her first trip on a boat, and it was wonderful.

As the sailing boat reached the edge of the lake an inquisitive duck swam across. Perhaps he thought Daisy was a slice of bread or a piece of tasty duckweed, for he grabbed her in his beak and hurried towards the shore.

But when he discovered that Daisy was no good to eat, he waddled out of the pond and dropped her in the long grass by the trees.

"Look! There's Daisy!" yelled Sam looking very relieved. "She must have been here all the time!"

"Promise you'll never, ever throw Daisy away again," said Sara holding onto her doll tightly.

Sam promised he wouldn't, but Daisy hoped he would. This was her first big adventure and she longed to have another one just as exciting!

Lawrence Goes Adventuring

On days when Lawrence woke up and remembered there was no school, he went ADVENTURING!

"I'm in the greenhouse today," he told his mum and dad.

"You're going ADVENTURING then!" they said smiling, and they opened the back door wide.

"Hat!" said Dad.

"Packed lunch!" said Mum. "Do try to be home for tea!"

Now it has to be said, greenhouses can be boring at times…but not this one!

Lawrence marched down the garden path to the greenhouse and flung open the door. In he strode, bold as could be…the noise was DEAFENING!

Squawking, squeaking, howls and hisses, growl, buzz, honk and ROAR!

"It's a jungle in here!" chattered a little monkey swinging down from a palm tree.

"Tell me about it!" replied Lawrence, failing to notice that a Giant Pincher Beetle had just landed on top of his hat.

"Time to cross the river," said Lawrence.

"Look out!" shrieked the monkey!

But Lawrence never saw the crocodile open its mouth wide, or heard its jaws close with a SNAP!

8

He was far too busy eating the egg and cress sandwiches his mum had packed for his lunch.

"Be careful, there's something hiding in the long grass!" warned the little monkey jumping up and down.

But Lawrence was enjoying his banana, and didn't even catch a glimpse of the tiger's sharp sparkling teeth.

Then Lawrence sat down on the steamy jungle floor and took out his last slice of cake.

"Ah, an elephant!" he cried. "Can you take me home in time for tea?"

"Don't move another step," whispered the little monkey quietly. "There's a giant snake sliding down from the tree."

But Lawrence didn't hear the snake hiss, he was trying to open his fizzy drink.

"He's back!" called Mum when she saw Lawrence fling open the greenhouse door.

"How was your adventuring?" Dad asked eagerly.

"Very quiet today," Lawrence replied, and went inside for his tea.

Tina and Twink, the Mermaid Twins

Tina and Twink were mermaid twins whose home was a beautiful coral reef, like a garden under the sea.

All kinds of creatures lived in the warm clear water around the reef. Every one of them loved the two little mermaids and went to visit them each day…this morning was no different…

First, a shoal of shimmering rainbow fish came by and wanted to play. Tina and Twink chased them and raced them all through the coral caves, until they caught up with them on the other side.

Then the tiny rainbow fish gathered into the shape of a heart – just for the two little mermaids.

"That's wonderful, you clever things!" said Tina blowing them bubble-kisses.

"Off you go, all of you!" laughed Twink clapping her hands. "We've something very important to do today."

10

And with a flick of their tails, the mermaid twins darted through the water, scattering the tiny rainbow fish in all directions.

Now earlier that morning, Tina and Twink had promised their music teacher they would practise tunes on their trumpet shells.

"We had better get started before any more of our friends call round to visit," said Tina, and both of the mermaids took a deep breath, ready to blow into their shells.

But right at that very moment, two rather friendly young turtles stopped by.

11

"Come for a ride to Seaweed Wood and see how fast we can go!" they called out to the mermaids.

"Sounds like a great idea!" cried Tina putting down her trumpet shell.

"It's better than practising tunes all morning," giggled Twink.

And with a flip and a flick of their mermaid tails, the mischievous pair leapt onto the turtles' backs and took off.

Both turtles whizzed through the water at tremendous speed, curving and swerving in and out of the swaying seaweed.

Very soon they completely forgot that the mermaids were riding on their backs, and they nearly flipped over a number of times.

"That was amazing!" gasped Tina and Twink when the turtles came to stop.

"Now we must go home and practise on our trumpet shells as we promised," said the little mermaids.

"But neither of the turtles could remember the way back!

"I'm afraid we're lost, and it's all our fault," said the poor turtles looking rather sorry for themselves.

"Don't feel bad," said Tina kindly. "It's our fault too, we should have stayed at home and practised."

"Let's play our tunes right now," suggested Twink, and she picked up one of the trumpet shells that lay on the seabed and began to play.

"It might make us feel better," sighed Tina, and she joined in with the music.

The two little mermaids played every tune they knew over and over again, and the turtles listened quietly.

All of a sudden they saw a bright shimmering flash, and the shoal of rainbow fish came darting out of the seaweed.

"Are you still practising your tunes?" asked the fishes altogether. "It's getting rather late. Time you two went home!"

With frisking tails and flips and bounds, the tiny fish gathered themselves into the shape of an arrow, and led everyone back to the coral reef.

"We kept our promise after all," said Tina when they were tucked up in their shells that night.

"I'm so glad we did," replied Twink drowsily. And the two little mermaids drifted off into a deep sleep.

13

The Wobbly
Spaceship

The spaceships of the Inter-galactic Star Fleet were ready at all times to be sent on vital missions across the galaxy.

As soon as the alarm sounded at their Control Base, they set off at hyper-speed through space.

For problems on planets, colliding shooting stars, runaway rockets or any astro-disaster, the spaceships of the Inter-galactic Star Fleet were always on hand.

But one spaceship was different from the rest!

At first he was sent on missions with the rest of the fleet, but it wasn't long before the other spaceships started to make fun of him.

"Wibble! Wobble!" taunted one .

"You're just like a jelly!" jeered another.

All this teasing made the poor spaceship feel very ashamed, because it was true…he did wobble!

For however hard he tried, he could not stay upright for long. First he flew to the right, then tilted to the left, and

14

more often than not, he would overbalance and start to spin.

He was indeed, a very wobbly spaceship!

And if that wasn't bad enough, he found it impossible to land…which is bound to happen if you wobble.

If ever he did manage to reach a planet, he would bounce across the surface like a pebble skimming over water. In a way that was lucky, because the wobbly spaceship always managed to avoid large rocks and missed falling into deep craters.

Other travellers in space got out of the way the moment they saw him flying unsteadily towards them.

"If my flying doesn't improve," said the spaceship sadly, "I'll be thrown out of the Inter-galactic Star Fleet!"

Then one day he was close to the Control Base when the alarm sounded. "Emergency! Emergency! A manned rocket has been reported missing for over a week. All spaceships return to base immediately!"

Swiftly the whole Inter-galactic Fleet assembled to hear their instructions.

"This is your most important mission so far," they heard the voice of their Base Controller say. "Search everywhere for the missing astronaut and bring him back safely. Good luck all of you!"

As the fleet of spaceships set off, one of them shouted to another.

"Wibble! Wobble! The Jelly will save him!" and the rest of them sniggered as they whizzed by.

Feeling very hurt, the wobbly spaceship set off a bit behind the others, for it was quite clear that they didn't want him around.

He searched the galaxy for hours and hours. Sometimes he flew to the right, then he tilted to the left, but all the time he kept a sharp lookout for the missing astronaut.

After flying for so long, the wobbly spaceship needed a rest and tried to land on a nearby planet. He bounced across the surface – as he always did – then he bumped into something hard and metal, but luckily came to a stop without a single scratch.

"You're here at last!" he heard a voice call, and standing there was the missing astronaut. "My rocket ran out of fuel and crashed here over a week ago. Am I pleased to see you!"

And with that, the astronaut jumped aboard the wibbly wobbly spaceship, took off from the planet and steered towards home.

The spaceship had never flown so fast or so straight before. He didn't tilt to left or right and he couldn't overbalance if he tried.

It felt just wonderful!

"All you needed was a pilot," laughed the astronaut. "Now all I need is a spaceship like you!"

So from then on, the two of them conquered space together.

Sadie Keeps a Secret

Every year when summer came around Sadie and her best friend, Phoebe, would go camping.

On the morning of their holiday it always took ages to pack everything they needed into Sadie's little car. The boot was so full of luggage they could hardly close the lid. Also squeezed into the back seat were a couple of skateboards, Phoebe's and Sadie's large tent, and a smaller one for Sadie's dog, Tippi.

The girls couldn't go on holiday and leave Tippi behind, could they?

Now best friends should always tell each other their secrets, don't you agree? But this year Sadie had a secret she wanted to keep from Phoebe…just for a little while.

"I must be taking a lot more clothes than last year," said Phoebe looking at all her extra cases.

"Me too," said Sadie bringing out more and more bags.

"We'll never get all this stuff in the car," Phoebe sighed. "I'll have to leave some of my clothes behind."

"No you won't," laughed Sadie as she fetched a huge sun umbrella and two tennis racquets.

"We're not leaving Tippi's new puppy behind, are we?" asked Phoebe with dismay.

"Don't worry," smiled Sadie. "They'll be plenty of room for her."

Phoebe shook her head. "There's no way everything will fit into your car," she said looking at the growing pile. Then she gave a little shriek. "We've forgotten the tents!"

"No need for tents any more," said Sadie mysteriously. "Look what's parked in front of the garage!"

Right next to Sadie's little car was a brand new camper van.

"Do you like the colour?" Sadie asked her best friend.

"I love it," gasped Phoebe. "How did you manage to keep it secret?"

"It was really hard," Sadie laughed. "Now let's pack the van and go on holiday!"

Farmer Barley's New Friends

Farmer Barley was busy in his fields all through the year, there was plenty of work to be done. He got up very early every morning and was always late to bed at night.

Most days Farmer Barley jumped in his tractor and drove off into the fields, but he never had anyone to talk to, except a lot of crows and a friendly-looking scarecrow.

At the start of the year Farmer Barley would plough the soil ready for setting seeds in the spring. And in summer, when the corn needed

cutting, he would climb up into his massive combine harvester and work until darkness fell, with only the owls to keep him company.

Although Farmer Barley enjoyed working on his large farm, he sometimes felt lonely.

Then one day, the farmer's wife came into the yard with a wonderful surprise for him.

It was a sheepdog!

"Thank you, my dear," said Farmer Barley. "I shall call her Meg. Now we must have some sheep for her to round up."

So the farmer bought some sheep.

"How about a cow or two for me to look after?" the farmer's wife asked – she could get lonely too, when the farmer was away in the fields all day.

So he went off to market and bought some cows.

"Little pigs would be nice!" Farmer Barley said as soon as he got home.

"Let's buy a goat," added the farmer's wife, "and don't forget a few hens!"

"Our farm will be even busier now," laughed Farmer Barley.

"And we'll never feel lonely again." said the farmer's wife.

I think she wanted lots of animals all along, don't you?

21

Princess Goldie and Geraldine

If you believe in wishes and enchanted fountains, then this story is for you…

Although Princess Goldie lived in a magnificent palace with countless servants, she often felt lonely. Her loving parents, the King and Queen, gave her everything she asked for, but what Princess Goldie wanted most of all was a friend.

Every day she would go outside into the palace gardens and play all alone by the fountain.

"I'll pretend this fountain is enchanted and make a wish," said the Princess out loud. So she closed her eyes tightly and, as you may have guessed…she wished for a friend.

Surprise, surprise, when the Princess opened her eyes, waddling across the lawn was a large white goose.

"At last, I have a friend!" cried Princess Goldie, and she ran towards the goose and gave her a great big hug. "I shall call you Geraldine, and we'll do everything together!"

And so they did.

Geraldine went to live with the Princess in the palace. The King and Queen were delighted and didn't mind a bit, and soon the goose became part of the royal family – they even had breakfast together.

The Queen fed Geraldine dainty slices of buttered toast, and the King gave her half his cereal that popped and crackled. Princess Goldie's favourite breakfast was a blueberry muffin, and now she shared it with her goose every morning.

The magnificent royal palace was full of empty rooms and endless corridors, can you think of a more perfect place to play?

For the very first time, the King and Queen heard whoops of joy from the Princess as she chased Geraldine all round the palace.

Sometimes the goose would chase the Queen, which made the King laugh until tears rolled down his cheeks, and he had to beg Geraldine to stop.

Princess Goldie's days were never dull again, for the goose made sure she had plenty of fun.

"I wish I could dance!" exclaimed the Princess one day. To her surprise Geraldine knew all the new steps, and showed her how they were done.

The King and Queen watched for a while then joined in. They hadn't danced for years, but they soon got the hang of it!

After breakfast one morning, when Princess Goldie and her goose had gone outside, the Queen said to the King, "We ought to give Geraldine a present, she has brought so much happiness to us all."

The King thought this was a wonderful idea and sent for the royal jeweller immediately.

The very next day, the royal couple presented Geraldine with a beautiful golden crown.

"For the best friend in the world!" Princess Goldie declared as she placed the crown on Geraldine's head.

Then one terrible morning, when Princess Goldie was late going outside after breakfast, she thought she saw Geraldine flying away.

"I must be mistaken," she cried racing across the lawn. The Princess called and called, but before very long the goose had flown from out of the palace grounds and disappeared beyond the trees.

"Perhaps it's not Geraldine," said the Queen trying her best to comfort her daughter.

"I will send every servant in the palace to look for her," the King promised when the goose hadn't returned by nightfall.

Where, oh where was Geraldine?

The weeks passed by, everyone searched high and low, but no trace of the goose could be found.

Poor Princess Goldie thought about Geraldine all the time. She couldn't sleep, and she didn't want to eat she was so unhappy.

"Our palace is awfully quiet," said the Queen, "you can almost hear a pin drop."

"No one dances any more now Geraldine has gone," the King sighed. "Soon I'll have forgotten all the steps."

And when the three of them sat down to breakfast each morning, nothing seemed the same. The Queen didn't want her dainty slices of buttered toast, and the King pushed away his bowl of cereal that popped and crackled.

Then one wonderful, magical morning everything changed!

When the princess saw her favourite blueberry muffin she had an idea. Quickly she grabbed the blueberry muffin off the plate, ran outside and stood by the fountain.

"I'll pretend this fountain is enchanted and make a wish," said the Princess out loud. So she closed her eyes tightly and, as you may have guessed…she wished that her goose would come back.

Surprise, surprise, when the Princess opened her eyes, Geraldine was busy pecking at the blueberry muffin…and right behind her were six golden goslings!

Princess Goldie was overjoyed, so were the King and Queen, and from that day on the palace was filled with noise and laughter once more…not to mention lots and lots of dancing!

Digby Clears the Road

Brad came running out of his office into the yard.

"I've just had a phone call, there's an urgent job for us!" he shouted to Digby, his yellow digger. "A pile of earth is blocking the main road into town. It needs moving right now!"

. Digby was busy shifting sand into a waiting dumper truck.

"Last scoop then I'm finished!" called Digby.

Once the dumper truck was full, it was about to pull away when Brad shouted across to Digby again.

"I'll just be a minute. I need to find my hazard jacket and put it on, this job could be dangerous and I need to be seen clearly."

Now the dumper truck heard everything Brad said. "This sounds exciting," he thought to himself. "I'll try to find out what's going on!"

When the dumper truck reached the site where the sand was needed, a cement mixer was parked nearby.

"A huge landslide has blocked the main road into town!" the dumper truck told the cement mixer excitedly. "They've sent for Digby, shall we follow him?"

"Count me in!" said the cement mixer starting up his engine.

Straight away the dumper truck tipped his load of sand, then the two machines moved off together.

Coming down the road towards them was a bulldozer with its blade off the ground.

"Listen to this!" yelled the cement mixer. "The mountain has fallen across the main road into town!"

"Sounds like a big problem," said the bulldozer. "There's bound to be lots of stones and huge rocks, not to mention massive boulders!"

"They've sent for Digby and we're following him," said the dumper truck.

"Wait for me!" cried the bulldozer . He didn't want to be left behind and miss all the excitement.

"Where are you lot going?" enquired a road roller as the dumper truck, the cement mixer and the bulldozer passed by.

"The mountains have fallen, there is rubble everywhere, and the main road into town is completely blocked. They've sent for Digby and we're following him!" gasped all three of the machines together.

"Mind if I tag along?" asked the road roller. "I move rather slowly, but I get there in the end." And he rumbled off behind them. When they reached the blocked road, Digby was already moving earth and Brad was putting out cones.

"How about a bit of help?" said Digby with a grin…he was very pleased to see the four machines. "There's a lot of earth to shift, and urgent repairs to be done before the road can be opened."

28

"That's why we followed you here," said the cement mixer.

"We were told that the whole mountain had fallen onto the road!" the road roller mumbled.

Brad looked puzzled. "Now where did you get that idea?"

The dumper truck kept quiet and so did the other machines. Every one of them had added a bit to the story and made things sound worse than they really were.

"You're all here now, so let's get started!" shouted Digby.

Before very long a van full of workmen arrived to lend a hand, and after a lot of hard work all the earth was moved, the cement mixer repaired the edge of the road and the roller flattened the ground… the main road into town was opened at last.

"Well done!" said Brad to all the machines.

"We made quite a team, didn't we?" laughed Digby.

29

Mabel's Terrible Temper Tantrums

Mabel astonished everybody with her terrible temper tantrums. She had to have her own way all the time, and if not, she would scream and scream and scream, and yell and bawl at the top of her voice…it was deafening!

Worse still, if she was really cross, she would jump up and down with temper, kick the furniture and slam the doors. This made the whole house shake so much, the neighbours thought it was an earthquake…and who can blame them?

Toys and books were thrown all over the room every time Mabel got mad, then the cat would dash under the table and the dog would follow double quick…it was scary to watch!

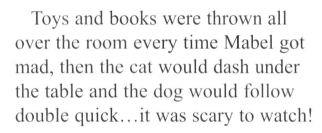

Mealtimes were a nightmare with Mabel at the table. She quite liked soup and small iced buns with cherries on top…but nothing else at all.

Did she eat her vegetables? Of course not!

Take cover, Mabel has been given a plateful of peas!

Then one day Mabel was taken to the zoo.

"I didn't want to come!" she screamed stomping past the penguins. "And I'm not going to look at any of the animals!" she yelled as she stomped past the chimps.

Perhaps an ice-cream might keep her quiet…and in a strange way it did.

Mabel took one lick and dropped it in front of the lion's cage…what a disaster!

She opened her mouth wide, took a deep breath – Mabel was about to have the most tremendous temper tantrum.

All of a sudden the lion moved to the front of his cage, he opened his mouth too, he took a deep breath, and gave an almighty ROAR!!!

The whole zoo trembled.

Very slowly, not making a sound, Mabel backed away and tiptoed past the lion's cage.

And from that day to this, she has never again had a temper tantrum.

In fact, she is the sweetest, gentlest, quietest little girl you could wish to know.

Eddie and Ted, Ghost Hunters

Late one night, by the light of the moon, Eddie and Ted went ghost hunting.

"Let's try over there," said Eddie pointing to Wailing Wood.

"This hollow tree looks spooky!" shouted Ted, and he banged on the trunk and stuck his head inside. "Come out, ghosts, we know you're there!"

"I bet they'll come out when they see me," said Eddie, who had brought along his Monster Mask.

Impatiently the boys waited and watched, but all they saw were a few vampire bats and the odd giant spider hanging from the tree.

"There's nothing much here," grumbled Ted.

"Then I think I'll go home to bed," muttered Eddie.

"Hold on!" said Ted. "I thought I heard a groan."

"Be quiet and listen," whispered Eddie. "I'm sure I heard a moan."

"WE KNOW YOU'RE THERE!" both boys hollered.

"SO COME OUT NOW!"

Ted, who always had his Master Beam Torch when he went ghost hunting, shone it up into the tree.

Low and behold, hiding in the branches were a whole family of ghosts.

"Go on, scare me silly!" ordered Ted.

"Please frighten me to death!" begged Eddie.

The ghosts looked embarrassed… one even turned red.

"Give us a few blood-curdling screams," pleaded Ted.

"Shriek, wail, screech…anything to scare us," begged Eddie.

The ghosts shrugged their shoulders and hung their heads.

"We don't know how to scare anyone," piped up the smallest one.

"You see, none of us have ever been taught how to scare properly," another ghost muttered. "I couldn't even frighten a mouse."

Eddie and Ted stared at the ghosts in disbelief.

"Your moans and groans sound like tummy rumbles!" and the two boys screamed with laughter.

The ghosts had to agree, and they all sighed quietly.

"What you need is A REALLY BIG SCARE!!!" yelled Eddie and Ted as loud as they could.

The ghosts clung to one another with fright.

"Meet us tomorrow," said Eddie and Ted mysteriously, "and we'll take you for a ride."

And so they did…in fact, the next day, the ghosts went on every ride, at Thunder Island theme park. Their shrieks, and wails and spine-chilling screams were terrifying to hear. Eddie and Ted were very proud of them.

So now…never go near Wailing Wood after dark, the ghosts in there are far too scary!

The Monster Behind the Fence

Francie loved her little dog Tasher, and Tasher loved Francie. When Francie was at home Tasher was happy all day long, but when she went off to school, Tasher was miserable. He would howl loudly as soon as she left the house. Then Francie's mum would put Tasher out into the garden so she could have a bit of peace and quiet.

Not that Tasher kept quiet! He would bark and yap, then yap and bark until Francie came home from school.

One morning, when Tasher had stopped barking for a minute, he discovered a hole in the garden fence and wriggled underneath.

"I've never been in a wood before," thought Tasher as he scrambled out on the other side of the fence. The woods looked so interesting, he forgot all about barking and yapping for once, and scampered towards the trees.

"Hi there!" a little brown rabbit called to Tasher. "You're new round here, come with me and meet a few of my best friends."

"An excellent idea!" replied Tasher, and without so much as a bark or a yap, he followed the little brown rabbit into the wood.

A grey and white badger poked his nose out of a deep hole, and a fox cub peeped out from behind a tree, a hedgehog stopped by to see what was

going on…each one had come to take a look at Tasher.

"It's so good to meet you all," said Tasher, who had always wanted to have some friends. "Strange I've never seen any of you before and I live close by."

35

"None of us go beyond the edge of the wood," whispered the badger. "We're all too frightened."

Tasher's tail stopped wagging at once.

"A terrible fierce monster lives there behind a garden fence," the hedgehog explained.

"There's a hole underneath the fence, and if ever the monster escapes, it will gobble up every single one of us!" the fox cub added.

Tasher pricked up his ears.

"None of us have ever seen the monster," said the little brown rabbit," but we can hear the scary noises he makes all day long."

Tasher looked puzzled. "I've never seen this monster, and I live behind the fence."

When Tasher heard how worried his new friends were, he began to bark very loudly. "I'm going to find this terrible monster and chase him away for you!" The little dog sounded so fierce.

In a flash, every one of Tasher's friends vanished, and he was left all alone.

Tasher stopped barking at once and looked round in surprise. Where had everyone gone?

After a while, to his delight, he saw the little brown rabbit hopping towards him with the others close behind.

"We've guessed who the monster is!" they shouted. "It's you!"

"Make that noise again!" cried the little brown rabbit eagerly.

"You mean barking," laughed Tasher, and he barked and barked until the sound echoed round the wood…and this time none of the animals ran away. Instead, one by one, they followed Tasher through the hole underneath the fence and scrambled into the garden.

When Francie got home from school that afternoon it seemed strangely quiet, Tasher wasn't barking as usual.

Straight away the little girl ran out into the garden, perhaps something was wrong. What if her little dog had run away?

Francie was astonished to find Tasher in the middle of the lawn with the animals from the wood. "You kept on barking because you felt lonely when I was at school," smiled Francie. "All you needed was a few friends!"

The Nacho Monster

"I feel like a snack," Ronnie said to his friend Rick one morning. "Something crackly, crunchy, crisp and munchy."

"Cornflakes?" asked Rick.

"That's not what I want at all," said Ronnie. "I want a snack in a great big bag so you can munch as you go down the street."

Then Rick started hopping from one foot to the other. "I know! I know!" he yelled. "A MONSTER BAG OF NACHOS!"

"That's exactly what I want," agreed Ronnie. "Now let's go and get some!"

So off they raced to the nearest supermarket and went straight to the shelves that held the snacks.

They found fifty different flavoured crisps, cheesy puffs, onion hoops, loop-the-loops, even potato sticks that tasted of sardines.

BUT NO MONSTER BAGS OF NACHOS!!!

"We've run out!" said the manager.

"Run out?" gasped Ronnie and Rick together. "A supermarket with NO MONSTER BAGS OF NACHOS! That's unheard of!"

"My biggest customer has just bought the lot," said the manager. "There he is going through the door."

"Who needs that many bags of nachos?" asked Ronnie.

"Let's find out," said Rick.

Once outside the supermarket, the boys stood still and stared.

"Tell me this isn't real," gulped Ronnie.

"Pinch me – I must be dreaming!" Rick's voice sounded ever so squeaky.

"HI THERE!" a loud voice boomed. Standing right in front of them was a Hairy Monster with a trolley full of MONSTER BAGS OF NACHOS!

"It's quite alright," the Hairy Monster assured them, "the manager lets me take the trolley home as long as I bring it back the next week."

"That's kind of him," squeaked Rick.

"He must be able to trust you," blurted out Ronnie.

Then the Hairy Monster pointed his paw at the trolley full of nachos. "We're having a party, do come and join us!"

Ronnie and Rick just nodded their heads, it's true to say they were lost for words.

"Hang on to my trolley!" the Hairy Monster boomed and took off like a rocket. "We'll go through the park, it's the quickest way back for me."

The three of them sped past the bandstand towards a clump of bushes.

"Help! Slow down!" both boys yelled and closed their eyes as they crashed through the bushes.

"Here we are," boomed the Hairy Monster. "Come and join the party!"

When Ronnie and Rick dared to open their eyes they were in the middle of a garden full of monsters of all shapes and sizes.

Balloons and streamers were everywhere, music was playing and there was lots of yummy, scrummy party food on the table.

"HERE COME THE MONSTER BAGS OF NACHOS!" boomed the Hairy Monster in a voice much louder than before, "AND I'VE BROUGHT ALONG TWO NEW FRIENDS!"

These monsters were a jolly lot… so Ronnie and Rick found. They loved to dance, play games and sing, but most of all…THEY LOVED EATING NACHOS!!!

And, as you know, so did Ronnie and Rick.

When all the nachos had gone and the party came to an end, Ronnie and Rick thought it was time for them to go too.

"Shall we take your trolley back to the supermarket for you?" the boys asked the Hairy Monster.

"No need!" he boomed "I'll be going there as usual next week to buy all the MONSTER BAGS OF NACHOS."

"Save some for us!" laughed Ronnie and Rick. Then they closed their eyes, and when they opened them, they were back in the park next to the bandstand.

If your supermarket runs out of MONSTER BAGS OF NACHOS every week...I'm sure you can guess were they've gone!

Will Anna Miss the Show?

Anna loved to dance. She went to classes two evenings a week and the whole of Saturday morning.

Like all of her classmates, Anna dreamed of becoming a ballerina.

Then one day Anna was given some very exciting news. Miss Sweetly, who taught her ballet class, had been asked to put on a show in a real theatre.

"You can all take part if you wish to," said Miss Sweetly smiling at the girls, "but we shall have to start practising right away."

Everybody in the class was thrilled and gathered round to be shown their new steps.

"I can see I'm going to be busy too," laughed the lady who played the piano for dancing.

Later when Anna returned home, she could hardly wait to tell her family.

"I'm going to dance in a beautiful costume on a real stage," she called as she flung open the front door.

Then, to her dismay, she tripped over a rug and fell and hurt her ankle…what a disaster!

Anna had to be taken to see the doctor without delay.

"You've bruised your ankle badly," he said. "There'll be no dancing for a week, but you will be fine in time for the show."

Anna was very upset to miss her dancing, but her mum promised to take her to Miss Sweetly's class, so she could watch the others and learn the steps.

That night as Anna was going to bed, she had a very clever idea.

"If I take my ballerina doll with me, and move her arms and legs into the right dance positions, it will help me remember my steps for the show."

Anna's idea worked brilliantly. After a week her ankle was better and she went back to Miss Sweetly's class.

"I'm amazed," Miss Sweetly gasped as she watched Anna dance with the others. "You know the steps of every dance perfectly, well done!"

The theatre was packed on the night of the show. The girls looked beautiful in their new costumes and danced like real ballerinas. Miss Sweetly was so proud of them for giving such a splendid performance.

Anna had never felt so happy, and that night she gave her ballerina doll a special hug for all her help.

A Whale of a Tale

Crystal Cove Harbour was so busy the Harbour master sent for his nephew, Chad, to give him a hand.

"I've never seen so many boats coming in and out," said the Harbour Master. "Everybody wants my help, and I can't be in two places at once."

"Don't worry, Uncle," replied Chad cheerfully. "I'll soon sort things out."

"A fishing boat has just tied up at the jetty. There's a problem with the engine!" Chad's uncle called as he hurried to find out what was the matter.

"IT'S ON FIRE!!!" yelled Chad, and he grabbed a bucket, filled it with water from the harbour, then threw it onto the smoke and flames.

Luckily it put out the fire straight away.

"Thanks a million, you've saved my boat," said the fisherman shaking Chad by the hand. "If the fire had

spread, it could have destroyed every boat in Crystal Cove Harbour."

Later that night, when all the boats had been safely tied up, Chad and his Uncle were walking along the jetty gazing out to sea.

"Look there, Uncle, a whale!" cried Chad pointing.

As his Uncle watched the whale spouting water, he came up with a clever idea.

"Crystal Cove Harbour needs a very special boat to do a very special job," he told Chad.

"I shall order one first thing in the morning."

Next day when the new boat arrived, it really was special.

"A FIREBOAT!" cried Chad as he jumped on board. "I know there isn't a fire, but can I try it?"

"Certainly!" laughed his uncle. All the boats that come into Crystal Cove Harbour will be safe from now on!"

45

Whitney the Witch

When Charlie went back to school one Monday morning he could hardly believe his eyes. Sitting at the desk next to him was a little girl dressed as a witch.

"Please take care of our new pupil," the teacher, Miss Plum, said to Charlie. "Her name is Whitney and she will be with us for the rest of the year."

"Do you always come to school dressed in that weird outfit?" asked Charlie the moment Miss Plum turned her back.

Whitney shrugged her shoulders and looked puzzled, "Every witch I know dresses like this."

"I don't believe it," Charlie sighed, "I have to look after a girl who thinks she's a real witch. Great!"

Charlie slumped down in his chair and put his head on the desk with a mighty thump.

"Ouch! That hurt!" howled Charlie as a big purple bruise appeared on his brow.

"This will make it better," said Whitney with a sweet smile. She tapped Charlie's head with her wand and the bruise vanished.

Right there and then Charlie knew she was a real witch, and that a real witch with a real magic wand could make school very interesting.

"Do I call you Witch Whitney?" asked Charlie.

"Just Whitney will do," the young witch replied unpacking her school bag.

As the weeks went by Charlie discovered Whitney was the cleverest of witches. She got top marks in every test, and her homework was always correct.

46

"Why do you bother doing any work at all?" Charlie asked Whitney one day. "Just wave your wand and your lessons will be done."

"That's strictly against the rules!" Whitney sounded quite shocked. "Witches must learn things for themselves and never use their magic at school."

"You made the bruise on my head disappear by magic," Charlie pointed out to her.

"That was an emergency," whispered Whitney.

Then one morning Whitney went into Miss Plum's office to have her books marked, and she left her magic wand on the desk.

Without thinking what might happen, Charlie grabbed the wand and pointed it at a computer, "Vanish!" he ordered…AND IT DID!

Not satisfied with that, he pointed the wand at a model of a dinosaur on Miss Plum's desk, "Come alive!" he ordered…AND IT DID!

As the dinosaur lumbered through the classroom it kept growing and growing. By the time it had crossed the hall and stepped outside into the playground…IT WAS ENORMOUS!!!

The bell for the morning break had just rung and the children had gone out to play.

"What is that?" shouted the big boys when they spotted the dinosaur.

"Is it going to eat me?" asked one of the little girls.

"He's a dinosaur, and he won't eat you because he's a vegetarian," said Whitney, who had just come out into the playground followed by Charlie.

"That's alright then!" yelled the children. "Come on, let's play with the dinosaur!"

Charlie looked sheepishly at Whitney. "Sorry for using your magic wand. Mind if I go and play with the dinosaur?"

To his amazement Whitney wasn't in the least bit cross. "I've broken the first rule of magic," she said. "You must always keep your wand with you at all times, so it's really my fault." Then she started to giggle, "I'm going to play with the dinosaur too!"

No one seemed to mind a dinosaur at school. Miss Plum took to him right away because he wiped his feet well on wet days, and kept the children quiet with his wonderful stories.

The dinosaur delighted the ladies who served the school lunch, he always ate up his greens, and so the children did too!

At the end of each day, when it was time to go home, Miss Plum had a golden rule, "The dinosaur must be back on my desk as soon as the home bell rings!"

Then Whitney would wave her magic wand and the dinosaur became a model once again.

49

Red the Rescuer

Big Joe and his mighty tow truck, Red, were always prepared for sudden emergencies. They would travel anywhere, any time, answering calls for help however difficult or dangerous.

Red and Big Joe's work began very early one morning. The bridge across the harbour was stuck fast, it had to be released before ships could pass through once more.

So Big Joe hooked up the crane, Red gave one powerful tug, and the bridge was open!

"Try and get that bridge mended today!" called Big Joe as they drove away.

Next came a major situation. A volcano, far beyond the mountains, was about to blow!

Taking great care, Red pushed a giant boulder over a cliff. Down the valley it hurtled, flew up and landed right on top of the volcano!

Well done, Red! You've saved the valley!

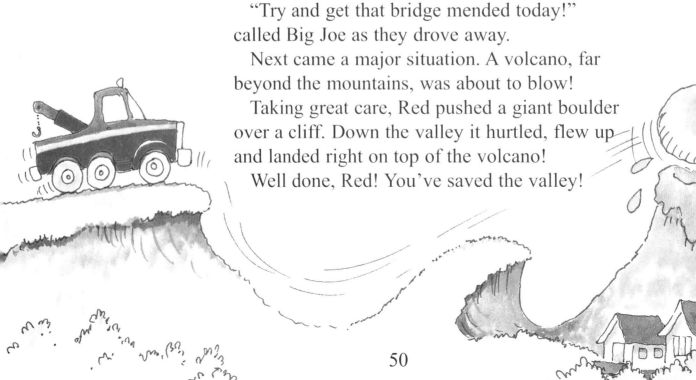

50

Big Joe and Red had no time to waste that day. A house was about to topple into the sea.

"Pull as hard as you can, Red," yelled Big Joe, "there are folks still inside!"

Red moved the house to safety and everybody cheered, "Thanks Red, you're the best!"

Then came the biggest job of the day.

"The Space Centre's transporter has broken down," said Big Joe, "and the launch is in less than one hour."

With his super strength, Red managed to drag the transporter and the Space Shuttle to the launch on time.

Countdown began…and in ten seconds Red watched with Big Joe as the Space Shuttle blasted off into space…we have lift off!!!

But was that their biggest job today?
Perhaps not!

A great herd of elephants had to be moved across an enormous park.

"I'm sure Red can do it," said Big Joe, "if they all promise to stand still and don't run away!"

Then on the way home Red began to cough and splutter. Big Joe quickly switched off the engine.

"I'll find out what's the matter," said Big Joe, and he jumped down from the cab, climbed on top of the wheel and opened Red's bonnet…there was a loud hissing sound and a cloud of white steam.

"A water hose is leaking." Big Joe sounded worried. "I'm sorry, Red, I haven't got a spare."

Big Joe and Red had been busy helping people all day, let's hope someone will help them now.

52

As Big Joe sat by the side of the road wondering what to do, a little boy rode up on his bicycle.

"What's the matter with Red?" he asked Big Joe.

"Leaking water hose," replied Big Joe.

"No problem," smiled the boy, and he reached into his pocket. "You can have my repair kit, I use it to mend my bike tyres."

"You're a boy in a million!" laughed Big Joe. "You can tell all your friends that today you rescued Red the Rescuer!"

Lilith's Fairy Dust Hat

Lilith, the littlest fairy, had lost her flower petal hat.

"I need a brand new one," she said, and flew off to look for a new one right away.

The littlest fairy picked the first flower she came to and popped it on top of her head.

"How do I look?" she asked a dragonfly that was hovering close by.

"As silly as can be!" he replied.

"Then how about a red poppy hat?" Lilith asked him when she had chosen another flower.

"Poppies make you sneeze, and by the way, you have a smudge of black pollen right on the end of your nose!" and he fluttered back to his home by the river tittering all the way.

Next Lilith tried a daisy hat, but it was far too heavy and a wee bit old-fashioned.

"I know!" cried the littlest fairy. "A foxglove bell would fit me just beautifully!"

But she was wrong. The hat was so big, Lilith was lost inside and had to call for help.

Now the Fairy Queen (who always knew what was happening to every fairy), was absolutely brilliant at choosing hats.

"For you, the softest thistledown," said the Fairy Queen, and with a wave of her magic wand, and a sprinkling of fairy dust… there was Lilith's new hat!

How it sparkled and twinkled, how it glittered in the sunlight.

"A perfect hat for my littlest fairy," said the Fairy Queen smiling at Lilith.

55

Grandad's Birthday Present

It was Grandad's birthday tomorrow and Archie's mum and dad were trying to think of a present.

"Chocolates would be nice," suggested Mum.

"We buy those every year," Archie sighed.

"How about a book on gardening?" asked Dad.

"Boring, boring, boring," groaned Archie.

"Then you think of something," said Mum and Dad together.

"A robot!" said Archie firmly. "Grandad would just love a robot!"

So off they droved to a huge toy store on the edge of town and bought a robot.

Archie took great care of it on the way home, and then gave Grandad the robot on his birthday morning.

"I've always wanted one of those robots," chuckled Grandad. "He can help me make things in my workshop!"

"Pardon?" said Mum frowning.

"What did he say?" said Dad.

"I just knew he'd love it," grinned Archie.

After Grandad had eaten three slices of birthday cake and read all his cards, he led the robot into his workshop and closed the door.

"Leave Grandad alone with his present," his mum told Archie. "You can come into the kitchen and help me with lunch."

As Archie peeled potatoes and chopped up carrots, he could hear the oddest sounds coming from his Grandad's workshop…hammering, tapping, clinking and clunking, and a noise that sounded like wings flapping or beaks snapping.

Archie could stand it no longer. He rushed out of the kitchen and thumped on the workshop door.

"Come in, Archie, and see what we've made," Grandad called from inside.

And when Archie opened the door…this is what he found!

Grandad and the robot had been very busy indeed.

"I knew you'd like the robot," Archie gasped as he stared around.

"It's the best!" grinned Grandad.

57

Jessie's Little Foal

When her pony, Candy, had a foal, it took Jessie ages to choose a name.

"She's so special," said Jessie when she looked into the stable the day the little foal was born. "I need to think of a really special name."

"How about Dasher, or Dancer or Prancer?" suggested her brother, just teasing.

"They're the names of Santa's reindeer," said Jessie, "so stop being silly!"

"You wouldn't let me choose the name anyway," shouted her brother, and he ran off leaving Jessie gazing fondly at the foal.

A whole week passed and still Jessie hadn't come up with a name, it was so difficult.

"Come along, sweetheart," Jessie said to the foal as she opened the stable door – that was the name she was using – just for the time being.

The little foal followed Jessie everywhere. When she was busy in the stable yard, the foal stayed close behind her. Sometimes she got in the way and jobs had to be done again, but Jessie didn't mind at all.

"You were only trying to help, sweetheart," smiled Jessie giving the foal a hug.

58

"I see you've still got your shadow with you!" her brother called to her from across the yard.

"SHADOW!" cried Jessie jumping up and down with delight. "Shadow is brilliant, I can't think of a better name!"

So, thanks to her brother, from then on the little foal was called Shadow, and on a day in summer she lived up to her name!

One weekend, a horse show was being held in a field near Jessie's home. She was taking along her pony, Candy, to compete in some of the events.

On the morning of the show Jessie got up earlier than usual. She needed plenty of time to groom her pony so she would look her very best.

Jessie fetched her brushes and began by cleaning Candy's coat, next she combed her mane and long flowing tail.

"Nearly done!" she said to Candy, and last of all, she oiled her pony's hooves and gave her coat a final polish with a sheepskin mitt.

"Now it's my turn to get ready," said Jessie, and she hurried into the house.

All this time Shadow had been trying to poke her head over the stable door, and when Jessie returned dressed up for the show, she couldn't resist going into the stable to give the foal a great big hug.

"Wish us luck, Shadow!" laughed Jessie. Then she saddled up Candy, rode out of the yard and galloped off to the horse show.

Before too long, Shadow began to miss Jessie and Candy and was anxious to see where they had gone.

To her surprise when she tried to poke her head over the stable door… it swung wide open!

Jessie was in a hurry and couldn't have closed it properly.

Out trotted the curious little foal, across the yard, past the rest of the stables and into the garden.

Now Shadow had never been in a garden before, and couldn't work out what it was for. So she rolled up and down the lawn and raced in and out of the flowerbeds.

Still looking for Jessie and Candy, Shadow managed to squeeze through the hedge, and then she set off down the lane towards the horse show.

Once through the main gate, she could see Jessie and Candy in the show ring, and a judge was presenting Jessie with a large silver cup.

A crowd was standing watching, and when they spotted Shadow entering the ring they all started to clap. The little foal thought this was great fun, so she tossed her head and bowed, and then trotted across the grass daintily.

As she reached Jessie and Candy, a voice over a loudspeaker announced, "This is the winner of the Prettiest Foal in the Show Competition!"

"That's you, Shadow! You've won first prize!" exclaimed Jessie taking hold of her foal's head collar.

When the show ended, Jessie led Candy and Shadow back home.

"This explains why you are covered in flowers," said Jessie as they walked passed the ruined flowerbeds.

But how could Jessie be cross with Shadow for following her and Candy to the show? None of this would have happened if Jessie had closed the stable door properly!

And Shadow did win first prize for the Prettiest Foal in the Show - so it all turned out quite well after all!

Pete and Branco, Range Riders

Pete lived on The Three Horseshoe Ranch and rode a horse called Branco.

Every year the town nearby held a rodeo and Pete went along to watch the contests in the ring. Folks came from near and far to see the cowboys test their skills. The rodeo show was always exciting and often very dangerous.

To begin with, there was bareback riding on broncos that bucked and reared. Some of the more daring cowboys tried riding bulls, and others jumped from their horses and wrestled steers to the ground.

When the time came for cattle-roping, Pete always pushed his way to the front of the ring, and climbed up on top of the fence to get a better view.

Pete had just been given his own lasso, he could do a few rope tricks, but nothing like the rodeo cowboys.

"I need lots of practise if I'm going to be a real cowboy," thought Pete as he headed back to the ranch, "then I'll be a rodeo star some day."

And how hard Pete practised! Every day he stood outside with his lasso, spinning the rope into small loops, large loops – even figures of eight.

"Time to try roping," said Pete out loud, and he tossed his lasso over the nearest fence post. "Right on target!" shouted Pete, very pleased with himself. So he tried once more… and did it again!

By the end of that morning he'd lassoed every fence post in the yard, and never missed one!

From then on, Pete lassoed everything in sight. One day he lassoed his grandma snoozing on the porch in the sun.

"Time to try roping on the move!" Pete declared, and he saddled up Branco and rode away.

Beyond The Three Horseshoe Ranch grew lots of giant cactus…just perfect for Pete to lasso.

"I'll never do it!" yelled Pete as Branco galloped past the first one at top speed… but he roped the cactus easily.

Sometimes Branco would swerve, just to make it harder, but Pete lassoed a giant cactus every single time.

"Time to rope my first steer," said Pete patting his horse's neck. Branco tossed his head and snorted loudly. Was this really a good idea?

Pete stood up in his stirrups and gazed across the ranch. A herd of cattle were grazing in the distance but they were too far away.

"We'll have to wait and rope my first steer tomorrow," Pete told Branco, and he pulled on the reins and headed for home.

On his way back to The Three Horseshoe Ranch, Pete and Branco had to cross a railway line. As they neared the track Pete was certain he could hear snorting and bellowing.

There, standing in the middle of the line, was a very angry looking bull.

"He's a long way from the herd," said Pete with dismay. "We're going to have to take him back."

When the bull spotted Pete and Branco, he stopped bellowing and at once began to paw the ground.

Suddenly a whistle blew!

"There's a train coming and the bull is in the way!" yelled Pete. "Come on, Branco, it's up to us!"

The whistle blew again and kept on blowing. This meant the driver had seen them and was trying to stop the train.

Would he make it in time?

Pete grabbed the lasso, swung it round twice then tossed it over the animal's head.

He's roped the bull! Hurrah!

Slowly and carefully Branco trotted away, pulling the bull behind him on the rope.

SCREEEECH! The train came to a halt just as the line was cleared.

Down jumped the driver looking very relieved. "You and your horse have saved my train and all the passengers. When we reach town the Sheriff will hear how brave you have been!"

Before they went home Pete and Branco led the bull back to the herd.

And when they rode through the gates of The Three Horseshoe Ranch, the Sheriff was waiting to thank them.

"One day, you'll be champion of our town rodeo," he laughed shaking Pete's hand, "and I'm sure you'll be riding Branco!"

Musical Party Dresses

Rosie, Gem, Tilda and Bridget dressed alike at school. They always wore their school uniforms, because that was the rule. But when they went to parties they liked to look different!

One afternoon when the girls arrived home from school, their mum had something exciting to tell them.

"You've been invited to a party," said Mum. "It's at five o'clock tomorrow, and you have to dress up."

The four girls shrieked. "We don't have any dressing up clothes to wear!" they cried, "and tomorrow is a school day!"

"No problem," said Mum. "I can go to the shops in the morning and choose some great outfits for you."

Rosie, Gem, Tilda and Bridget ran to their mum and gave her a hug, then they all stepped back and took a deep breath.

"I want to go as a princess," said Rosie.

"I want to go as a ballerina," said Gem.

"I want to go as a mermaid," said Tilda.

"And I want to go in a sparkly dress," giggled Bridget.

Next morning Mum went off to the shops, and much later came back with loads of parcels.

The four girls talked about the party all day at school, and came home feeling very excited.

When Mum unpacked the dresses, Rosie, Gem, Tilda and Bridget were thrilled to bits.

"I don't know which one to choose," said Rosie.

"Nor do we," said Tilda and Gem.

"They're all so sparkly," giggled Bridget.

The four girls couldn't decide what to wear, and they changed their minds several times.

Mum, however, knew exactly how to solve the problem. She put the dresses into a large bag and switched on some music.

"Pass the bag round, girls!" she shouted. "When the music stops, the one holding the bag puts her hand inside and pulls out a dress for the party."

The first time the music stopped, Rosie was holding the bag. "Great!" she cried. "Mine's the mermaid costume!" and she passed the bag on.

When the music stopped again, it was Tilda this time. "Brilliant!" she laughed, "I've got the ballerina's dress!" and she passed the bag on.

Gem was next when the music stopped. "Wow!" she gasped. "I'm going dressed as a princess!" and she passed the bag on to Bridget. Hers was the last dress of all, and when she put her hand in the bag, she pulled out the final costume.

"Mine is the sparkliest one of all!" she giggled.

The bag was empty, and Rosie, Gem, Tilda and Bridget were ready to go to the party.

67

Tod, the Strongest Toddler in the World

When Tod was a baby he could kick and crawl, play peek-a-boo, wave bye-bye, touch his nose with his toes, lie flat on his back…AND JUGGLE WITH HIS BIG BROTHER!!!

And everyone said, "He must be the strongest baby in the world!"

In a little while, when Tod was a toddler, he could do a lot more… stretch up high and bend down low, play ring o'roses, walk on tiptoe…but when he went for a ride on his trike…HE PULLED EVERYBODY ALONG TOO!!!

There was Teddy in the truck,
Ginger on the train, his best friend
Hank riding the horse, Rags in the
trolley, Kitty in the doll's pram,
Bret balancing on his skateboard,
the baby-sitter in the trailer followed
by Tim's red car, Tod's sisters in
fancy dress going to a party, Mum
reading, Dad relaxing… Tod could
pull them all along easily.

And everyone said, "HE MUST
BE THE STRONGEST TODDLER
IN THE WORLD!!!"

Don't you agree?

An Invitation to a Party

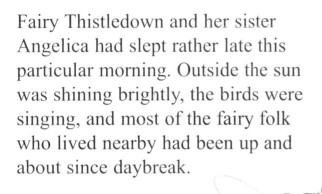

Fairy Thistledown and her sister
Angelica had slept rather late this
particular morning. Outside the sun
was shining brightly, the birds were
singing, and most of the fairy folk
who lived nearby had been up and
about since daybreak.

"Don't hold me up, I'm in a hurry!"
the bumblebee buzzed crossly.
"Special delivery, sign here, please!"
He thrust a letter through the open
window and off he sped.

"It looks like an invitation," yawned
Angelica still drowsy.

A velvet-coated bumble-bee with a
satchel by his side had been tapping
on Thistledown and Angelica's front
door for ages. He was just about to go
away when he noticed that the fairies'
bedroom window was wide open, so
up he flew. The sound of his noisy
buzzing awoke the two sleeping
fairies, and they looked out of the
window in surprise.

The letter was written on a rose petal tied with a cobweb covered in dewdrop pearls.

"It's from the Fairy Queen," gasped Thistledown, who by now was wide-awake. "We've both been invited to a party at the palace…and it's today!"

Angelica, still in her fairy nightclothes, fluttered round the bedroom shrieking, "We haven't got a thing to wear! We haven't got a thing to wear!"

"Of course we have," said Thistledown calmly. "Our wardrobe is full of party dresses." She was a bit older than Angelica and could always solve any problem.

"I'll never be able to choose one in time for the party," wailed Angelica still fluttering round.

"Then let me choose for you," said Thistledown trying to be helpful. "I suggest your white organdie one trimmed with gold lace."

"Of course!" cried Angelica, "I'll wear my satin slippers with the green ribbons."

"Perfect!" agreed Thistledown. "I'll go in lavender and palest pink speckled with sparkling beads."

"That sounds perfect too," laughed Angelica and she rushed over to the wardrobe to find their dresses.

There is so much to do when you are going to a party – bracelets to find, necklaces to try on, and what about your hair?

It took the two fairies all morning to get ready…they even forgot to have lunch.

Every time Thistledown and Angelica went to a party, the butterflies in the garden pulled their fairy carriage made of plaited ribbons covered with flowers.

"I'll find out if the butterflies are ready!" called Thistledown as she went outside.

"And I'll check what time we should arrive at the Fairy Queen's palace," said Angelica reading their invitation.

Suddenly Thistledown heard a tiny scream and Angelica came flying out into the garden. "Our invitation is for this evening, and not this afternoon," and the shocked fairy read out loud,

72

Thistledown knew how to solve the problem, and flew off to talk to the butterflies.

When she came back she was smiling. "Don't be sad," she told Angelica. "Everything is arranged, we can go to the party tonight."

While Angelica dried her eyes, Thistledown popped inside the house and made her sister some of her favourite elderflower waffles, just to cheer her up.

And that evening, when it was dusk and the first stars began to twinkle in the sky, their carriage arrived at the door pulled by silver-winged moths…who were the butterflies' cousins!

They even brought a few fireflies along to light Thistledown's and Angelica's way to the palace. Problem solved!

"You are both invited to the Fairy Queen's Dusk till Dawn Party at the Palace."

At once both fairies realised that the butterflies couldn't possibly pull their carriage at night, for they folded their wings as soon as the sun set, then slept all night until dawn.

Poor Angelica started to cry, she felt so disappointed. Thankfully

The Pirate Twins

Ollie and Matt were identical twins. They looked alike of course, but they never dressed the same...except when they were playing pirates. Then it was impossible to tell one from the other.

One day Great-gran came for a visit. "Call yourselves pirates, boys?" and she tittered. "Real pirates always wear eye patches!" and she pulled a couple out of her handbag.

"Brilliant!" cried Ollie.

"Cool!" cried Matt.

"Be prepared, both of you," smiled Great-gran, "strange and exciting things will happen when you wear them," and she settled down in an armchair for a nap.

The instant Ollie and Matt put on the eye patches, they whizzed high in the air surrounded by showers of sparks and a cloud of blue smoke. Round and round they whirled, then plunged downwards and landed with a thump.

"Where on earth are we?" gasped Ollie.

"On the deck of a ship," replied Matt quietly, "and it's a pirate ship!"

"That's impossible!" said Ollie trying to keep his balance as the ship moved with the waves.

All that Matt could do was stare. "Look at those cannons, and this ship is flying the Jolly Roger!!!"

"There's no land in sight," called Ollie running to the ship's rail and gazing out to sea.

But his twin brother didn't reply, for a powerful hand had grabbed him by the shoulder.

"Stowaway aboard, captain!" yelled an evil-looking man as he dragged Matt across the deck.

Ollie quickly hid behind a barrel trying to think what to do next.

When Matt looked up, standing before him was the most fearsome man he had ever seen. He was the terror of the high seas…Captain Blackheart.

"Stowaway, eh?" he growled. "He's come to steal our treasure more likely. Rope him to the mast where I can keep my good eye on him!"

While the pirates were tying up his twin brother, Ollie crept across the deck and climbed up the rigging – that way he could see what was happening.

As Matt struggled to get free, he noticed that the deck of the ship was littered with doubloons and pieces of eight that had spilled out of a large chest.

"He's seen pirate gold, boys!" shouted Captain Blackheart, "and you all know the punishment for that!"

"Make him walk the plank!" yelled the crew angrily.

Was that really going to happen to poor Matt?

Time for some quick thinking by Ollie. He decided to play a trick on the pirates…identical twins play this kind of trick on people all the time!

As Matt set foot on the plank, Ollie shouted down from the rigging, "This ship is doomed if you make me walk the plank!"

This made Captain Blackheart and his crew shake with fear as they stared up at Ollie.

"That boy is bewitched!" screamed one of the pirates. "He can fly!"

Matt, meanwhile, had jumped down from the plank and was standing in the middle of the deck.

When the pirates noticed him, their faces went pale with fright.

"If any harm should befall me," Matt spoke in his scariest voice, "you and your ship will roam the high seas for all time."

Just at the right moment, Ollie jumped down from the rigging and stood next to his twin, Matt. Seeing them together was too much for the pirates, and they fled in all directions.

"We tricked them, didn't we, Matt?" laughed Ollie. "And I think I've figured out the way to get home.

Great-gran's eye patches brought us here, they'll take us back again!"

So Ollie and Matt pulled off their eye patches immediately, and in a shower of sparks and a cloud of blue smoke, they whizzed through the air and landed with a thump right next to Great-gran's armchair.

"Met Captain Blackheart and his pirate crew, then?" asked Great-gran giving the boys a knowing wink.

"We sure did!" Ollie and Matt replied, and both of them pulled a golden doubloon from their pockets and handed them to Great-gran.